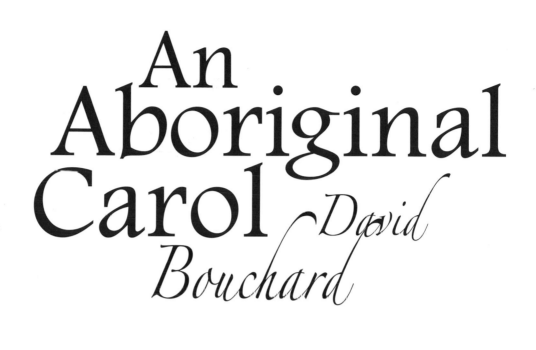

An Aboriginal Carol

David Bouchard

For my beautiful wife Vicki. For ten magical years!
David Bouchard

With thanks to the continued support of the Ontario Arts Council.
Moses Beaver

*Special thanks to my mother Dorothy for her direction and knowledge
and also to Jean Kusugak for her assistance. Thank you.*
Susan Aglukark

Published by
Red Deer Press
A Fitzhenry & Whiteside Company
1512, 1800–4 Street S.W.
Calgary, Alberta, Canada t2s 2s5
www.reddeerpress.com

Credits
Sound Design and Mastering by Geoff Edwards – streamworks.ca
special thanks to the following musicians:
Flute, Barbara Prowse, David Bouchard; Elk Skin Drums, Grahame Edwards
Design by Wycliffe Smith Design Inc.
Printed and bound in Canada by Friesens for Red Deer Press

Financial support provided by the Canada Council, and the Government of Canada
through the Book Publishing Industry Development Program (BPIDP).

Library and Archives Canada Cataloguing in Publication
Bouchard, David, 1952-
An aboriginal carol / David Bouchard ;
illustrations, Moses Beaver ; music, Susan Aglukark.
Poem.
Based on: Jesous ahatonhia written by Jean de Brébeuf.
To be accompanied by a CD-ROM.
For children.
ISBN 978-0-88995-406-9 (bd.)
I. Beaver, Moses, 1960- II. Aglukark, Susan III. Title.
PS8553.O759A75 2007   jC811'.54   C2007-905342-4

CANADA'S FIRST CAROL

An Aboriginal Carol

David Bouchard

ILLUSTRATIONS BY MOSES BEAVER

TRANSLATION AND MUSIC BY SUSAN AGLUKARK

Red Deer PRESS

"ACCORDING TO TRADITIONAL FIRST
NATIONS KNOWLEDGE AND BELIEF, JESUS
CHRIST WAS REINCARNATED BEFORE
CONTACT BETWEEN THE WHITE EUROPEAN
AND THE WENDAT (HURON) PEOPLE.

JESUS WAS KNOWN AS DEGANAWIDEH,
THE PEACEMAKER. HE BROUGHT
THE KAYENEREHKOWEN OR GREAT
LAW OF PEACE TO THE HODENAUSAUNEE
OR IROQUOIS.

Moses Amik S.I.B./06

AN ABORIGINAL CAROL, KNOWN AS
THE HURON CAROL, IS ABOUT THE ONE
JESUS CHRIST...BORN IN BETHLEHEM
AND BORN AGAIN AMONG THE
UHKWEHUWEH OR 'TRUE-HEARTED PEOPLE.'"

CANADA'S ABORIGINAL PEOPLE
CONSIST OF THREE GROUPS:
FIRST NATIONS, INUIT AND MÉTIS.
THIS COLLABORATION IS THE PERFECT
AMALGAMATION OF THESE THREE GROUPS...

'TWAS IN THE MOON OF WINTERTIME
WHEN ALL THE BIRDS HAD FLED
WHEN SQUIRREL WAS NESTLED IN HIS BED
WHEN GRIZZLY SLEPT...I HEARD IT SAID
BEFORE THE WHITE MAN HAD YET TO COME
WHEN DARKNESS CALLED FOR FLUTE AND DRUM
IT WAS THE DEAD OF WINTERTIME
WHEN ALL THE BIRDS HAD FLED

ᐅᑭᐅᕐᒍ ᓂᑭᐳᒍ
ᓐᖕᒦᐊ ᓐᒡᐋᕐᖁᐳ
ᓯᖁᕐ ᐃᓂᒻᓚᕐᕈᒪᓐᓗᒡ
ᐊᖅᓗ ᕯᓂᖅᓗᓐᖅ
ᐅᖅᖁᒦ ᔪᖁᐊᖅᐳᖕ
ᖃᑉᓱᓂ ᓐᑭᖅᖁᖅᓇᓕ
ᐅᖕᖁᐊᖅᒡ ᕿᓚᐅᕐᓇᖅᕐᓐᓗᒍ
ᐅᑭᐅᕐᒍ ᓂᑭᐳᒍ
ᓐᖕᒦᐊ ᓐᒡᐋᕐᖁᐳ

THAT MIGHTY GITCHI MANITOU
SENT ANGELS CHOIRS INSTEAD
AND DRUMMERS FROM ALL NATIONS CAME
AND SINGERS WITH BUT ONE REFRAIN
AND DANCERS FROM ACROSS THE LAND
THEY CAME TOGETHER HAND IN HAND
WHEN MIGHTY GITCHI MANITOU
SENT ANGELS CHOIRS INSTEAD

ᐊᑕᓂᖅ ᐊᑕᓂᕐᔪᐊᖅ
ᐊᐃᖏᓪᓕᕐᓂᒃ ᑎᓕᑦᓯᕗᖅ ᐃᒻᖏᓕᖅᐸᑦ
ᕿᓚᐅᔭᖅᑏᑦ ᓄᓇᒥᐅᓕ'ᒪᑦ ᑲᑎᑉᐳᑦ
ᐃᒻᖏᖅᑏᑦ ᐃᒻᖏᖅᑐᑦ ᐊᑕᐅᓯᕐᒥᒃ
ᒧᒥᖅᑏᓪᓗ ᓄᓇᓕᖕᓂᖖᒑᖅᑐᑦ
ᑕᓯᐅᖅᓗᑎᒃ ᑲᑎᓚᐅᖅᐳᑦ
ᐊᑕᓂᖅ ᐊᑕᓂᕐᔪᐊᖅ
ᐊᐃᖏᓪᓕᕐᓂᒃ ᑎᓕᑦᓯᕗᖅ ᐃᒻᖏᓕᖅᐸᑦ

BEFORE THE ANGELS STARS GREW DIM
AND WONDERING HUNTERS HEARD THEIR HYMN
ONE MYSTIC FLUTE - ONE HUNDRED DRUMS
ONE MESSAGE CLEAR, "A KING HAS COME!"
NOT ONE HAD EVER SEEN THE LIKE
BY LIGHT OF DAY OR MOON OF NIGHT
BEFORE THE ANGELS STARS GREW DIM
AND WONDERING HUNTERS HEARD THIS HYMN

ᐊᐃᖕᑊᑖᑦ ᖃᐅᒪᓇᖕᑦ ᐸᖕᕆᕐᐊᖃᖕᑎᓐᓕᑦ
ᐊᖏᓇᔨᑦᒍᑦ ᑐᖏᖕᒍᑦ ᐃᓕᖕᑊᑐᓂᑦ
ᓇᖕᖕᒐᖕᑦᒍᑦ, ᑐᖕᖓᖕᑦᒍᑦ ᖅᑲᐅᑎᖏᑦ
ᑐᑭᓇᖕᕐᕪᑦ, "ᑯᓯᐊᖕᑐᕐ ᑎᑭᒪᑦᒙ"
ᑕᑯᖕᖃᐅᕐᕐᒥᓕᖕᑦᓕᖕ ᑖᐃᒪᐃᑐᒥᖕ
ᐅᕈᐳᖕᑦ ᐅᖕᓄᐊᕐᖕᖕᓄᑦ
ᐊᐃᖕᑊᑖᑦ ᖃᐅᒪᓇᖕᑦ ᐸᖕᕆᕐᐊᖃᖕᑎᓐᓕᑦ
ᐊᖏᓇᔨᑦᒍᑦ ᑐᖏᖕᒍᑦ ᐃᓕᖕᑊᑐᓂᖕ

JESUS YOUR KING IS BORN

JESUS IS BORN

IN EXCELSIS GLORIA

ᔪᕐᔅ ᑯᕝᐃᐢᑐᕐ, ᐃᕐᓂᐊᖕᐅᖑᖅ

ᔪᕐᔅ ᐃᕐᓂᐊᖕᐅᖑᖅ

ᓂᖅᑐᖅᑕᐅᓕ ᒍᑎ

WITHIN A LODGE OF BROKEN BARK
A TENDER BABE WAS FOUND
A LONE ABANDONED TIPI
IN THE BUSH, A CHILD WAS FOUND
A SACRED SMOKE PAINTED THE SKY
BOTH WOLF AND OWL STOOD WATCH NEARBY
WITHIN THIS LODGE OF FUR AND BARK
A NEWBORN BABE WAS FOUND

ᐃᑉᖴᓇᒃᑦᐳᐊᑕᒥᒼ
ᓄᑕᕋᑋᖅ ᓇᓂᖝᐅᕋᖅ
ᖀᒪᖝᑕᐅᕈᖅ ᑐᐱᖅ
ᓇᐅᕋᖅᑐᓂ ᓄᑕᕋᖅ ᓇᓂᖝᐅᕋᖅ
ᐃᕈᐟᒍᖝ ᖀᓚᕋᒥᐧᒍᐧᖀᖅᑐᒻᒼ ᓇᓇᐃᖅᑕᐅᑊᓄᓂ
ᐊᒪᕈᖅ ᐅᖅᐱᑊᓪ ᒥᐊᓂᖅᔪᐧ
ᐃᑉᖴᓇᒃᑦᐳᐊᑕᒥᒼ
ᐃᓅᕐᖅᑐᖅ ᓄᑕᕋᑋᖅ ᓇᓂᖝᐅᖅᒪᒼ

A RAGGED ROBE OF RABBIT SKIN
ENWRAPPED HIS BEAUTY ROUND
HIS MOTHER HOVERED OVER HIM
HER GENTLE VOICE; THE ONLY SOUND
HIS FATHER BY THE FIRE STOOD
HE'D FOUND SOME FOOD - HE'D BROUGHT
    SOME MORE WOOD
A SIMPLE ROBE OF RABBIT SKIN
ENWRAPPED HIS BEAUTY ROUND

ᐅᑲᓐᐅᑉ ᐊᖔᓄᑦ
ᐃᓂᑦᑕᓇᖕᑫᖕᒡ ᐃᒡᔾᖅᒡᒐᔭᖅ
ᐊᓀᑕ ᒦᐊᓂᐤᖦ
ᓂᐱᑯᒍᐊᒍ ᑐᖕᖅᖕᐅᐟᔾᒡᓄᓂ
ᐊᒡᒡᓗ ᐃᑯᐊᒡᖅᒍᐟ ᖁᓄᐊᓂ ᓇᖕᖅᖅᐳᖅ
ᑕᒡᐊᖕᖕᓄᖕ ᓇᓂᔭᖅ, ᖃᔪᑖᖅᔪᓄ
ᐅᑲᓐᐅᑉ ᐊᖔᓄᑦ
ᐃᓂᑦᑕᓇᖕᑫᖕᒡ ᐃᒡᔾᖅᒡᒐᔭᖅ

Moses Amik s.L.B 07

AND AS THE HUNTER BRAVES DRAW NIGH
THE ANGELS SONG RANG LOUD AND HIGH
FROM SEA TO SEA ALL NATIONS STOOD
THEY HEARD THIS SONG - THEY UNDERSTOOD
IT'S SAID THAT MAN AND BEAST AWOKE
TO SEE WHAT VOICE IT WAS THAT SPOKE
JUST AS THE HUNTER BRAVES DREW NIGH
THE ANGELS SANG THIS LOUD AND HIGH

ᐊᖑᓇᓱᒃᑐᑦ ᖃᓂᒡᓕᖕᒪᑕ
ᐊᐃᖏᓪᓛᑦ ᐃᒻᖏᖅᑐᑦ ᑐᓴᕐᓇᖅᓯᕗᑦ
ᓯᓚᕐᔪᐊᕐᒥᐅᓕᒫᑦ ᓇᖏᖅᑲᑎᒌᒃᓗᑎᒃ
ᐃᒻᖏᐅᑎᒥᒃ ᑐᓴᖅᐳᑦ - ᑐᑭᓯᐊᓕᖅᓗᑎᒃ
ᐅᖃᖅᑐᖃᓚᐅᖅᓯᒪᔪᖅ ᐃᓄᐃᑦ ᓂᕐᔪᑏᓪᓗ ᑐᐸᓚᐅᕐᓂᖏᓐᓄᑦ
ᑕᑯᓯᐊᖅᓗᑎᒃ ᑭᓇ ᓂᑉᓕᕐᒪᖔᑦ
ᐊᖑᓇᓱᒃᑐᑦ ᖃᓂᒡᓕᖕᒪᑕ
ᐊᐃᖏᓪᓛᑦ ᐃᒻᖏᖅᑐᑦ ᑐᓴᕐᓇᖅᓯᕗᑦ

Moses Amik s...ℸ 07

JESUS YOUR KING IS BORN

JESUS IS BORN

IN EXCELSIS GLORIA

ᐳᐸᕐ ᑯᕠᐃᑦᑐᕐ, ᐃᕐᓂᐊᖕᒍᑭᖅ

ᐳᐸᕐ ᐃᕐᓂᐊᖕᒍᑭᖅ

ᓂᖅᑐᖅᑕᐅᓂ ᒍᑎ

O CHILDREN OF THE FOREST FREE
O SONS OF MANITOU
AND DAUGHTERS OF ONE LOVING GOD
THIS HOLY CHILD - HE SENT TO YOU
THIS IS A NIGHT TO DANCE AND FEAST
FOR WITH THIS CHILD COMES LOVE AND PEACE
FOR CHILDREN OF THE FOREST FREE
CHILDREN OF MANITOU

ᓇᐹᖅᑐᒥᐅᑦ ᓄᓇᒥᐅᑦ
ᐊᑕᓂᕐᔪᐊᖅ ᐃᕐᓂᖏᑦ
ᔫᑎᐅᑉᓗ ᓇᒡᓕᖕᓂᐅᑉ ᐸᓂᖏᑦ
ᐃᑉᔪᕐᓇᐃᑦᑐᖅ ᓄᑕᕋᖅ - ᐃᓕᑉᓯᓐᓄᑦ ᑐᓂᔭᖓ
ᐅᓐᓄᒃ ᒧᒥᖅᑕ ᕐᑯᕕᐊᓱᖅᑲᑎᒦᒃᑕ
ᐆᒪ ᓄᑕᕋᐅᑉ ᓇᒡᓕᖕᓂᕐᒥᑦ ᓴᐃᒪᓂᕐᒥᑦ ᐊᐃᒃᑐᕐᒫᑎᒍᑦ
ᓇᐹᖅᑐᒥᐅᑦ ᓄᓇᒥᐅᑦ
ᐊᑕᓂᕐᔪᐊᑉ ᓄᑕᕋᖏᑦ

Moses Amik S.L.B '07

THIS HOLY CHILD OF HEAVEN AND EARTH
IS BORN THIS DAY FOR YOU
A GREATER GIFT HE COULD NOT GIVE
HE FREELY GIFTS HIS SON TO YOU
A CHILD TO OPEN HEAVEN'S DOOR
THAT YOU MIGHT LIVE FOREVER MORE
THIS HOLY CHILD OF HEAVEN AND EARTH
IS BORN THIS DAY FOR YOU

ᐅᓇ ᐃᑉᔪᖅᓇᐃᑦᑐᖅ ᓄᑕᕋᖅ ᕿᓚᖕᒥᐅᑦ ᓄᓇᒥᐅᑦ
ᐃᖅᓂᐊᖑᕗᖅ ᐱᑉᓗᑎᑦ
ᐊᖏᓂᖅᓴᒥᒃ ᖃᐃᑎᔪᓐᓇᖏᓚᖅ˙˙
ᐃᖅᓂᓂ ᑐᓂᕚ
ᕿᓚᖕᒨᓯᓐᓇᖅᑯᑉᓗᑕ
ᐃᓅᔪᓐᓇᖅᑯᑉᓗᑕ ᑕᐅᕗᖓᓗᒃᑖᖅ
ᐅᓇ ᐃᑉᔪᖅᓇᐃᑦᑐᖅ ᓄᑕᕋᖅ ᕿᓚᖕᒥᐅᑦ ᓄᓇᒥᐅᑦ
ᐃᖅᓂᐊᖑᕗᖅ ᐱᑉᓗᑕ

COME, KNEEL BEFORE THIS RADIANT BOY
WHO BRINGS YOU BEAUTY, PEACE AND JOY
BEAR WITNESS TO HIS ONLY SON
RAISE UP YOUR VOICES - SING AS ONE.
COME THANK YOUR MAKER FOR THIS DAY
ACCEPT HIS GIFT - THAT HE MIGHT STAY
COME, KNEEL BEFORE THIS RADIANT BOY
WHO BRINGS YOU BEAUTY, PEACE AND JOY

ᓯᕐᑯᖅᑐᓇᑦ ᓯᕗᓂᐊᓄᑦ ᑖᑉᓱᒪ ᓄᑕᕋᐅᑉ ᐃᓂᕐᑯᓇᖅᑑᑉ
ᑐᓂᒫᑎᒍᑦ ᐃᓂᕐᑯᓇᕐᓂᕐᒥᑦ, ᓴᐃᒪᓂᕐᒥᑦ ᕐᑯᕕᐊᓱᖕᓂᕐᒥᓪᓗ
ᑕᑯᕗᒍᑦ ᐃᕐᓂᑐᐊᖕᒐᓂᒃ
ᓂᐱᖅᑯᖅᑐᓯᕆᐊᕐᓗᓯ ᐃᒻᖏᓇᕐᓯ ᐊᑕᐅᑦᓯᒃᑯᑦ
ᖃᐃᒋᑦ ᕐᑯᔭᓕᓗᒍ ᒎᑎ ᑖᑉᓱᒥᖕᖓ ᐅᑉᓗᕐᒥᒃ ᖃᐃᑦᓯᖕᒪᑦ
ᑐᓂᕐᕿᓯᐊ ᑎᒍᓗᒍ - ᐊᐅᓪᓚᕐᑯᓇᒍ
ᓯᕐᑯᖅᑐᒃᕖᕆᓚᕗᑦ ᐃᓂᕐᑯᓇᖅᑑᕐᕙᐊᖅ
ᑐᓂᒫᑎᒍᑦ ᐃᓂᕐᑯᓇᕐᓂᕐᒥᑦ, ᓴᐃᒪᓂᕐᒥᑦ ᕐᑯᕕᐊᓱᖕᓂᕐᒥᓪᓗ

JESUS YOUR KING IS BORN

JESUS IS BORN

IN EXCELSIS GLORIA

ᐳᔪᕐ ᕳᕒᐃᑦᑐᔮ, ᐃᑦᓂᐊᕐᎫᕿᖅ

ᐳᔪᕐ ᐃᑦᓂᐊᕐᎫᕿᖅ

ᓂᖅᑐᖅᑕᐅᓕ ᒻᑎ